ZIBBY PAYNE

& THE WONDERFUL, TERRIBLE TOMBOY EXPERIMENT

Zibby Payne & the Wonderful, Terrible Tomboy Experiment
Text © 2006 Alison Bell

Published in 2008 by Lobster Press™
1620 Sherbrooke Street West, Suites C & D
Montréal, Québec   H3H 1C9
Tel. (514) 904-1100 • Fax (514) 904-1101 • www.lobsterpress.com

Publisher: Alison Fripp
Editors: Alison Fripp & Meghan Nolan
Editorial Assistant: Morgan Dambergs
Graphic Design & Production: Tammy Desnoyers

We acknowledge the financial support of the Government of Canada
through the Book Publishing Industry Development Program (BPIDP)
for our publishing activities.

We acknowledge the support of the Canada
Council for the Arts for our publishing program.

The Canada Council | Le Conseil des Arts
for the Arts | du Canada

Library and Archives Canada Cataloguing in Publication

Bell, Alison
        Zibby Payne & the wonderful, terrible tomboy experiment /
Alison Bell.

(Zibby Payne)
ISBN-13: 978-1-897073-39-1
ISBN-10: 1-897073-39-9

        I. Title. II. Series: Bell, Alison Zibby Payne.

PZ7.B41528Zi 2006   j813'.6   C2005-907638-0

Printed and bound in the United States.

To my daughter, Elizabeth

– Alison Bell

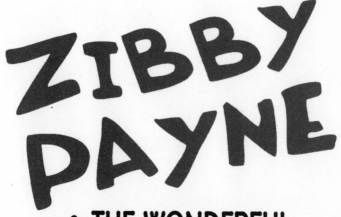

ZIBBY PAYNE

& THE WONDERFUL, TERRIBLE TOMBOY EXPERIMENT

Written by

Alison Bell

Lobster Press™

CHAPTER 1

NO ORDINARY MORNING

Today was unlike any other day in Zibby Payne's life. Today was her first day as a sixth grader.

"My friends and I are going to have the best year ever," Zibby said to herself as she gulped down a bowl of Cheerios for breakfast. Sixth graders received more privileges than the other grades, plus everyone in the school looked up to them.

She quickly dragged a brush through her shoulder-length hair, checking the clock one more time to make sure she wouldn't be late. She then kissed her mom goodbye, raced out of her house, and practically ran the three blocks to Lincoln Elementary. That was another great thing about being in sixth grade – her parents had decided to let her walk on her own to school, something she'd been begging to do for years.

Once she got there, she met up with her Absolute Best Friend on the Entire Planet, Sarah, out on the blacktop.

"Sarah!"

"Zibby!"

The girls hugged as if they hadn't seen each other in years, even though they'd spent the evening before together, organizing their school binders.

"Give me twenty!" they said in unison, and then performed the secret greeting they'd made up over the summer.

"High five high, high five low, clap your hands together," the girls shouted out while making the corresponding hand motions. "Spin around, touch your knees, reach for the trees, and give me ten!"

The girls collapsed into giggles. But then Sarah's face fell.

"Zibby," she pointed down at Zibby's shoes. "You forgot!"

Zibby and Sarah had planned on wearing one of each other's shoes – something they'd been doing since second grade because they'd always worn the same shoe size and liked the same styles. So there was Sarah, wearing one of her own sequined slip-ons on one foot, and on the other foot, one of Zibby's purple suede loafers, while Zibby was wearing clogs.

"I'm sorry. I guess I was too excited about the first day of school to remember," Zibby apologized. "Let's do it tomorrow instead, okay?"

"Okay, but don't forget again," said Sarah.

Just then their two friends, Amber and Camille, joined them. When Zibby saw them, her eyes almost fell out of her head! They usually wore jeans or shorts and long T-shirts, but today they were dressed up in denim miniskirts and fitted little T-shirts that barely covered their stomachs.

"What happened to you?" asked Zibby. "Did you make a wrong turn, thinking this was the high school?"

"Back-to-school shopping spree," Amber and Camille said together, spinning around to show off their outfits. Zibby's mom had also taken her shopping, but Zibby had bought capri pants, flared jeans, a few longer skirts, and some loose-fitting shirts. In fact, she was wearing new capris and a pink-and-purple-striped cotton T-shirt today.

"So what do you think?" asked Amber.

"I think you can't move or someone will see your underwear," said Zibby.

"That's why we wear shorts underneath," said Amber, raising up her skirt to reveal black cotton shorts.

"Very clever," said Zibby, glancing at Sarah, who was dressed in the same style as Zibby was. "Now Sarah, why didn't we think of that?"

"Because my mother would kill me," said Sarah. "She says I can't wear miniskirts until I'm thirty."

Amber pulled a little pot of something out of her backpack and spread it over her lips until they were very shiny.

"Is that makeup?" asked Zibby.

"Just some lip gloss," Amber shrugged. "'Groovy Grapilicious.' Want some?"

"No thanks," said Zibby. "My lips are fine the way they are."

The final bell rang, and the four girls lined up in front of their classroom. Once inside and sitting in their assigned seats, their teacher, Miss Cannon, gave a speech about "her expectations" of the class.

"No talking, no whispering, no passing notes, no contributing to class discussions unless you raise your hand," Miss Cannon droned on.

Why not just add no breathing or swallowing while you're at it, thought Zibby. *If teachers had their way, kids would sit as calm and still as robots.*

"And of course, since you're sixth graders now, we'll expect more out of you," Miss Cannon said. "You'll have homework every night – even on the weekends and holidays."

Zibby groaned to herself.

"However," continued Miss Cannon with a smile, "to make up for the extra work, you also get longer recesses and lunches. So enjoy."

Zibby smiled. *Finally, something to get excited about.*

Miss Cannon spent the first part of class passing out textbooks and outlining the year's curriculum. When the recess bell rang, Zibby practically bolted from her chair. She rushed outside and met her friends underneath the big eucalyptus tree near the blacktop.

"Tetherball, anyone?" asked Zibby, nodding to the two tetherball courts beyond the blacktop. Tetherball was her favorite thing to do during recess, probably because she always won.

"In this skirt? I don't think so," replied Camille.

"But you've got shorts underneath," Zibby pointed out.

"We're sixth graders now," said Amber, smoothing her hair and pulling out some more "Groovy Grapilicious" lip gloss. "We don't play tetherball or run around like fifth or fourth graders. We hang. That's what sixth graders do."

"What do you mean, hang?" asked Zibby, narrowing her eyes.

"Sit on the benches and talk and stuff," said Amber.

"Yeah, you know, hang," said Camille.

Zibby frowned.

Sixth grade was supposed to be the most fun ever, not the most boring, she thought to herself.

Sarah turned to her. "I guess we could try."

Zibby started to say "No way," but changed her mind. She didn't want to be a spoilsport on the first day of school.

"Okay," she said, trying to sound enthusiastic.

The four girls sat down on the benches. Amber, Camille, and Sarah started talking about some new guy group called BB5. Zibby had never heard of them. She never listened to pop music. She and her fifteen-year-old brother, Anthony, listened to classic rock, like the Beatles and the Eagles.

"What do you think, Zibby?" Sarah asked her. "Do you like their song, 'Baby You're Hot?'"

"Never heard of it," she said, thinking, *but that sure is a lame name for a song.*

"The one who's really hot is that lead singer, Tony," said Amber. "He's so cute. Have you checked out their web site? You can download pictures of him performing at their concerts. My mom said she'd help me blow one up into a poster!"

"Can she make one for me?" asked Camille.

"Me too?" asked Sarah.

Zibby rolled her eyes. She put her hands together and looked up toward the sky.

Oh dear Patron Saint of Sixth Graders, she inwardly prayed, *don't let me get stuck talking about boy bands and Groovy Grapilicious lip gloss every day at recess or I'll crumple up and die!*

She then looked off into the distance, watching a group of sixth-grade boys playing soccer on the grass field adjacent to the blacktop. They looked as if they were having fun. So did the fifth and fourth graders playing tetherball.

Zibby sighed. All summer long she'd looked

forward to sixth grade, but what a big mistake that was turning out to be. Because if school kept going the way it had gone today, sixth grade was going to wind up being the Absolute Worst Year ever!

CHAPTER 2

ANTHONY LOVES ASHLEY?

That night, Zibby was sitting at the dining room table trying to solve a math problem. Her mom sat at the other end of the table, jiggling Zibby's three-year-old brother, Sam, on her knees as she folded laundry.

Math was usually pretty easy for Zibby, but not tonight. Her thoughts kept drifting back to how disappointing the first day of school had been. Plus, the math problem made no sense at all to her!

"Listen to this," said Zibby to her mom in an exasperated voice. "If thirty darns equal six yarns, and twenty-four yarns equal twelve farns, how many darns make one farn?"

"Are you sure you're reading the problem correctly?"

"Yes," said Zibby, rolling her eyes. "The teachers make up these crazy math problems just to make sure we have a miserable sixth-grade year."

"Zibby," her mom said. "Calm down. I know if you slow down and read the problem again carefully, you can figure it out."

"I can't believe Miss Cannon gave us homework on the first day of school." Zibby shook her head in disgust. "I hate sixth grade."

"I'm sure it will get better," her mom said reassuringly.

Zibby sighed and looked at the math problem again, when the phone rang. She ran into the kitchen to grab it, but Anthony suddenly appeared out of nowhere and snatched the phone off the receiver.

"Hey, I was here first," she protested.

Anthony glared at her, clutching the phone to his chest as if it were precious treasure, then ran up the stairs.

"What's with him?" Zibby asked her mom, sitting back down at the dining room table.

"I think it's a girl calling," Zibby's mom replied.

"A what?"

"A girl. Ashley Gabler. Remember, a few weeks ago, a group of them went to the movies? Ashley was one of the girls. I think she likes Anthony."

"Really?" Zibby tugged at her ear as if she hadn't heard her mom correctly. *How can a girl like Anthony?* Sure, he was a really nice brother, but would any girl like him if she knew he hated to take showers, wadded up small pieces of paper and chewed on them like bubble gum, and burped every time he drank a soda?

"Are you sure?" she asked doubtfully.

Her mom nodded her head. "I talked to Ashley's

mom about it. I guess they've been instant messaging each other a lot and the other day, they met at Sir Juice-A-Lot for a smoothie."

"They went on a date?" Zibby asked incredulously. "Doesn't it bother you that Anthony's dating? I mean, isn't he kind of young?"

"He's fifteen, Zibby," her mom replied. "He's not *that* young."

Her mom folded the last shirt and scooped up the clean clothes into her arms.

"Sam, you come with me," she said. "And Zibby, you need to get back to your homework. If you're still having trouble, I can help you or you can ask Dad when he gets home from work."

Zibby nodded and tried again to concentrate on darns, farns, and yarns, but just then, Anthony came running down the stairs and into the kitchen to return the phone. Zibby jumped up and joined him in the kitchen. She and Anthony were very close, and told each other almost everything that was happening in their lives. She wanted to ask him if what her mom had said was true.

"Was that a girl on the phone?" she asked.

"No," he replied gruffly. "That was Joey, asking about science homework."

"Mom said it was someone named Ashley," Zibby persisted.

"Well she was wrong," Anthony snapped angrily.

"Quit bugging me, would you?" He charged out of the room.

Zibby shook her head, feeling hurt. Anthony hardly ever got mad at her. So her mom must be right – that must have been Ashley on the phone. Only a girl could make him so cranky.

Yuck, she thought. She just couldn't picture Anthony as someone's boyfriend. And the idea of him getting lovey-dovey with some girl made her feel sick.

On the other hand, Zibby thought, as she opened up the refrigerator and pulled out some juice, *the relationship was bound to be short-lived*. Once Ashley got to know Anthony, she'd see he was way too immature to date anyone. Zibby had read somewhere that the average teen romance lasted three weeks. She'd give this relationship more like three *days*.

The phone rang again and she snatched it up quickly.

"Ashley?" she asked, as she still had this mysterious "Ashley" on her mind.

"No, it's Sarah. Who's Ashley?"

"This girl that Anthony likes," exclaimed Zibby. "He went on a date with her – and she called him. Can you believe it?"

"No way," said Sarah. "Anthony has a girlfriend?"

"I know, it's totally weird," said Zibby. "But I think they'll break up any day now, so it's probably not a big deal. What's up?"

"I'm calling to tell you to bring some scrunchies and hair clips to school tomorrow," said Sarah excitedly. "We're doing hair! And don't forget about the shoes, either. My mom's calling me – got to go." And she hung up.

Doing hair? "What is Sarah thinking?" Zibby asked herself. They never "did" hair. That was the Most Boring Thing To Do On Earth. She and Sarah did fun things, like play tetherball, skip rope, and dance to Beatles songs.

Zibby slammed the phone down onto the receiver. "Just great," she said to herself sarcastically, wondering if she'd *ever* like recess again.

CHAPTER 3

SCRUNCHIES & SOCCER

"I don't see why you're all making such a big fuss about hair," said Zibby a few days later at morning recess – the third day in a row her friends had wasted a perfectly good morning recess primping. "It's just a bunch of dead skin cells growing out of your skull."

"Gross," said Amber.

"Ditto," said Camille.

Sarah looked hurt. "You always said my hair was pretty." She ran her hand through her blonde curls.

"It is," agreed Zibby. "But that doesn't make fixing hair any less boring."

"Oh, don't be a grump," Sarah said teasingly. "Let me put your hair into a low bun."

"A bun? I've never worn a bun in my life," Zibby said as she backed away.

"Oh come on Zibby, they're very *in* right now," replied Sarah. "All the movie stars have them. Here, let me try." She swooped up Zibby's hair in the back and secured it with an army of bobby pins and scrunchies.

Sarah leaned back and surveyed her work.

"There," she said, satisfied. "You look very glamorous."

"Just what I always wanted to be," said Zibby dryly.

Meanwhile, Amber and Camille were discussing a new reality TV show about a high school football team.

"Can you believe how cute the quarterback is?" asked Amber.

"Mega-cute," agreed Camille.

Amber and Camille launched into a discussion about who on the show was cute, who would be cute if they had better haircuts, and who would never in their entire lives be even a teensy-weensy bit cute, so why were they on the show anyway? Zibby tried to catch Sarah's eye to give her a "can you believe this?" look, but Sarah actually looked interested in the conversation.

Zibby had nothing to contribute. She just rolled her eyes and fidgeted with her hair. When Sarah went to the bathroom, Zibby saw her chance to save her appearance. She crawled underneath the bench, pretending to look for something she'd dropped, and quickly undid the bun.

"Sorry," she apologized when Sarah returned. "It just fell out!"

As they walked back to class, Zibby grabbed Sarah by the arm and took her aside.

"How can you take it?" Zibby asked. "Isn't all this

hair stuff and talk about boys driving you crazy?"

Sarah linked her arm through Zibby's as she always did when they walked together. "Amber and Camille are acting a little silly, but they're still our friends," she said reasonably. "We've known them forever. I'm sure they'll start acting more normal soon."

"I don't know if I can wait that long," said Zibby.

In fact, she didn't know if she could wait another recess. Back in class, she decided she would have to do something other than "hang" during afternoon recess. But what?

Some sixth-grade girls swung on the swings at recess. Zibby could join them, but swinging seemed too babyish. She could stay inside the classroom and help Miss Cannon file papers and organize lessons. *Nah*, she decided. *Too teacher's pet-ish.* Or she could play tetherball with the fourth and fifth graders. But they were just little kids, and she was a sixth grader. *Or*, she thought, *I could play soccer with the sixth-grade boys.*

Of all the options, that sounded the best. She used to play soccer every fall, and one year she'd made All-Stars. And even though girls usually never played, the boys had to let her in the game because the school had an "everyone plays" rule.

Okay, Zibby decided. *Soccer, here I come!*

During afternoon recess, she passed by the benches where she usually met her friends, and instead walked over to the field where the boys were gathering.

"Hey Matthew," she called out to a tall boy with brown hair and blue eyes. Matthew was the best athlete in the class. He also happened to be a total brainiac.

"Can I play?" she asked.

"No," he said dismissively, then kept on talking to the boys as if Zibby weren't there. "I'm one captain, Zane is the other. Zane can pick first."

Zibby tapped Matthew on the shoulder to get his attention. "School rule. Everyone plays," she said firmly. "And I want to play."

Matthew looked at her for a second, then snorted. "In those shoes?" He pointed downward.

Zibby looked at her feet. She'd forgotten she wasn't wearing tennis shoes. Today she'd swapped shoes with Sarah, and was wearing one of her loafers and one of Sarah's. *Oh well*, she thought. *True soccer talent doesn't need the right shoes.* But she made a mental note to wear her tennis shoes the next day.

"Don't worry," she said. "I can still play."

"All right," said Matthew reluctantly. He turned away from her and called out to Zane who was standing a few feet away. "Zane, you take Zibby as well as one extra boy." He looked back at Zibby. "You're going to need an extra player to make up for her."

Zibby rolled her eyes. "Girls can be good at soccer too, you know," she said huffily.

"Yeah, right," said Matthew, turning his attention back to choosing teams.

Once the teams were chosen, Zibby lined up with her team to receive the kickoff. Matthew kicked the ball from the center of the field, and Zibby rushed up to get it. She was just about to put her foot on the ball when another boy on her team, Steven, swooped in front of her, stole the ball from her, and dribbled down the field.

"Not fair," Zibby called out, but no one listened.

Over and over again during the game, she tried to get to the ball, but every time she was about to kick it, a boy hogged it from her.

I might as well be a leaf or clump of grass, she thought grumpily. *I'm totally invisible.*

But then, just as she was considering walking off the field, she got a lucky break. As she was standing down by her team's goal, the ball rolled her way and hit her foot before any of the boys on her team could take it from her. Zibby dribbled the ball toward the goal a few steps and took a shot. The ball went in the goal!

"Yeah!" screamed Zibby. She jumped up and down and waved her arms. The boys, however, didn't say anything. They just stared at her.

The bell rang, and recess was over. As Zibby walked off the field, Matthew fell into step alongside her.

"Good goal," he said, giving her arm a little punch, before running up ahead of her and catching up with some of the other boys.

"Thanks," said Zibby, smiling bigger than she had in days. She had scored a goal *and* gotten a compliment. *This has been the Very Best Recess of my life*, she thought to herself.

Just then, she saw Sarah standing along the edge of the field.

"Sarah," she called, rushing over to her. "Did you see me score that goal? Wasn't it great?"

"I saw it," said Sarah. "It *was* really good." But something about the tone of her voice didn't sound very enthusiastic.

"You okay?" Zibby asked.

"I'm fine," Sarah said, and then turned away from Zibby, putting her hand above her eyes as if she was looking for someone. "Oh, there are Amber and Camille – I need to talk to them." She ran off to where the girls were standing over by the classrooms.

That was weird, thought Zibby. *If Sarah thought my goal was so great, why did she run away like that? Doesn't she want to hear more about the game? And why did her voice sound so funny?* She shook her head, wondering about Sarah's reaction all the way back to class.

CHAPTER 4

SOMETHING TO THINK ABOUT

The next morning at school, Sarah arrived at the blacktop with shiny lips.

Zibby couldn't believe her eyes. When she got close up to Sarah and sniffed, she smelled grape.

"You've gone over to the dark side!" she exclaimed.

"It's just lip gloss," Sarah said, looking a little embarrassed. "It's not like real makeup or anything. It protects your lips from chapping. That's all."

Amber and Camille showed up then, and Amber was carrying a plastic purse filled with nail polish.

"Look what my mom bought me yesterday – a manicure set! We can do each other's nails today at recess," she said as she happily twirled her case in the air.

"Neat," cried Sarah. "What colors do you have?"

Amber opened the case. "Bubblegum Pink, Dazzling Berry, and Passionate Purple."

"I think I'll try Bubblegum Pink," said Sarah. "What about you, Zibby – which do you want to try?"

"Uh ... none," said Zibby. "I was going to play soccer again with the boys at recess."

"Again?" Sarah asked, sounding surprised.

"It was really fun," she said. "I had a blast."

"I just didn't know you were going to do it every day," said Sarah.

She pulled Zibby aside so the other girls couldn't hear what she was saying. "The thing is," she said, "I miss you. I like being with Amber and Camille, but it's just not the same without you there."

"I miss you too," said Zibby, even though she had to admit that she really hadn't thought about Sarah at all during the game yesterday. "It's just that I don't like hanging out – I'd rather play soccer. It's nothing personal against you, though."

Sarah sighed.

"I have an idea!" said Zibby, wanting to cheer up her friend. "You can play soccer *with* me. We'll do it together."

"But you know I'm a total klutz," exclaimed Sarah. "I'm terrible at soccer! There's no way I could ever play with the boys."

Zibby had to admit that Sarah had a point. When it came to sports, Sarah had two left feet – or more like three.

"How about if I play today with the boys during morning recess, but I promise to hang with you guys at afternoon recess?" Zibby suggested.

"Okay," said Sarah, brightening. "And I promise

that hanging out will be more fun from now on."

When donkeys fly, Zibby thought to herself. But not wanting to hurt Sarah's feelings, she just smiled and said, "I hope so."

Zibby ran onto the field at morning recess, ready to play. Unlike yesterday, today Matthew smiled and looked happy to see her.

"I'll take Zibby on my team," he said. And this time, he didn't take another boy to "make up" for Zibby.

Zibby beamed.

This time, things were different on the field too. Matthew passed the ball to her a few times, and so did Zane, who was on her team today. And once, Zibby drove the ball down the entire field, shot, and just missed the goal by a few feet.

"Good try," said Matthew.

"Way to go," said Zane.

She couldn't believe it! She was keeping up with the boys – and they were accepting her as a player. *This is the Second Greatest Recess of My Life*, she thought to herself.

She could hardly wait to play again during afternoon recess – until Sarah dropped by her desk and reminded Zibby of her prior commitment. "Ready to hang with us during second recess?" Sarah asked. Zibby's heart fell. *Ugh!* She'd promised to spend time with Sarah. And if she didn't, Sarah would feel hurt.

During afternoon recess, she tried her hardest to have fun. She let Sarah paint her nails Passionate Purple, and didn't even roll her eyes once when the other girls talked about how cute the group BB5 was again.

But still, her heart wasn't in it. She really wanted to be playing soccer with the boys.

As Matthew came off the field, he stopped in front of the girls. "Missed you out there, tomboy," he said, giving Zibby another one of his playful punches on her arm.

Zibby glowed. She'd been missed! But what was that he'd called her? *A tomboy? Hmm.* She'd never thought of herself as one before.

Is it an insult? she wondered. *Is he saying something's wrong with me because I'm doing something different from the other girls at recess?*

Or maybe it was a compliment. Maybe this was Matthew's way of saying she was a good soccer player, and that the boys liked playing with her. That she *was* different – but in a good way.

"Tomboy," she repeated to herself. She had to admit, something about it sounded right.

CHAPTER 5

ZIBBY'S BIG DECISION

For the rest of the day, Zibby pondered Matthew's comment.

Was she really a tomboy? And if she wasn't one, should she be?

What did she know about tomboys? They dress like boys and like sports. They wear their hair in ponytails, and don't wear makeup or nail polish. And they probably don't sit around blabbing about how cute TV stars or boy bands are. Tomboys are athletic and strong. And they aren't interested in boys ... at least not in *that* way!

Zibby didn't like wearing makeup or nail polish. And she liked to play sports. And she didn't like boys that way.

So maybe she was sort of a tomboy. That explained why Sarah, Amber, and Camille seemed so interested in things she didn't care about.

Just then, Zibby got one of her Very Good Ideas. If she already liked tomboy things, wouldn't it be a good idea to become even more of a tomboy? Then no one would expect her to sit around having her hair fixed or putting on gloppy lip gloss. They'd automatically know that tomboys didn't do such things. Then she could do just what she wanted. She'd never have to sit through another boring recess again in her life.

"That's it," she decided. "I'll become a tomboy. A total tomboy. It's the only way to save sixth grade."

Now she had to do what she always did when she came up with a Very Good Idea: tell Sarah about it. She always told Sarah everything first.

She ran over to Sarah's house, which was only a few blocks away, and gave her personalized rap on the door – three rapid taps, a short pause, and then a fourth knock. After a few seconds, Sarah appeared.

"Hi, Zibby," she said, smiling and throwing the door open. "What's up?"

"I've figured something out!" Zibby exclaimed. "Something that will make sixth grade the best year ever!"

Zibby rushed inside and sat down on the family room couch. Sarah sat next to her.

"What is it?" Sarah asked. "Tell me!"

"I've decided I'm a tomboy."

"A tomboy?" Sarah looked confused.

"You know – the type of girl who runs around playing sports with the boys and doesn't care about what she looks like. I've decided that's who I am."

"You just decided right now?"

"You know how I am, Sarah. When I make up my mind, I make it up quickly. And I've made up my mind that I'm the perfect tomboy."

Sarah frowned. "So you *are* going to spend every recess with the boys?"

"Well, tomboys have to play sports at recess – it's kind of like one of the rules," said Zibby.

Sarah's frown deepened.

Zibby wracked her brain, trying to come up with a way to present her idea without upsetting Sarah any more than she already had.

"But just because I spend recess with the boys doesn't mean I won't still do a lot of things with you," she continued. "We can still get together after school and on weekends. We'll still be best friends. So nothing will really change."

Sarah kept frowning. "What about shoe swapping? Can we still do that? Even if you're a tomboy?"

Zibby had forgotten all about shoe swapping. Sarah was totally into it – in fact, she'd been the one to first think of it back in second grade. She always said that Zibby had cuter shoes than she had and this way, every time Zibby got a new pair, it was as if she did too.

But there was no way Zibby could keep swapping shoes with Sarah now that Zibby was a tomboy. How could she kick a soccer ball wearing skimpy sequined sandals or pink clogs?

"I don't think we *can* still swap shoes," she said, trying to explain the situation as gently as possible. "The problem is, most of your shoes are too girly. I guess we could switch tennis shoes, but it's hard to run and play soccer in mismatched shoes, so that probably wouldn't work either."

Sarah looked as if she might cry. Zibby desperately thought of a way to make it up to her.

"We can still do our special secret greeting," she said. "Hey, let's do it right now!"

Sarah ignored her. But then she started to smile and said, "I know what I'll do. I'll start swapping shoes with Amber."

"Amber?" Zibby said. "Her feet are twice as small as yours, plus she thinks shoe swapping is gross because she says everyone else's feet stink!"

"You're right," said Sarah thoughtfully. Then her face lit up. "I'll swap with Camille then. We wear the same size. And she has really cute shoes!"

Zibby felt relieved that Sarah could still continue on with the shoe swapping, but she was also a little jealous that Sarah could so suddenly decide to swap shoes with someone else.

"Aren't her feet smaller than yours?" she asked.

"No – they've gotten bigger," said Sarah. "We're a perfect match."

Suddenly, Zibby's good tomboy news didn't feel

that terrific anymore. But she cheered herself up by thinking about how much fun she was going to have on the soccer field tomorrow.

Just then, Sarah's mom called from the back of the house. "Dinner!"

"I guess I have to go," Sarah shrugged.

The girls stood up.

"Thanks for filling me in," said Sarah.

"You're welcome," said Zibby, heading for the door.

"Oh, and Zibby?"

"Yeah?" Zibby turned back around.

"I'm happy for you," Sarah said, smiling. "I know you were miserable sitting around at recess."

"Thanks," Zibby said, giving her a quick hug.

But as she walked home, she wondered just how happy Sarah really was. Because just as Sarah closed the door, she'd seen something flit across Sarah's face. Something that didn't look happy at all. Not one little bit.

CHAPTER 6

NOTHING TO WEAR

That evening, Zibby thought about how to launch her official Tomboy Transformation. The first step, she decided, was to purge her closet of anything frilly, foufy, sophisticated, girly, or uncomfortable.

"From now on," Zibby declared, "I will only wear clothes I can play soccer in."

She threw open her closet door. Some of her back-to-school clothes still had tags on them. Zibby yanked each piece of clothing, old and new, off their hangers and scrutinized them one by one to see if anything was tomboy worthy.

"A pink-and-white striped T-shirt with a butterfly on it? Yuck!" she said out loud as she threw the shirt on the floor.

"Ruffled skirt for 'special occasions.' Gone." She tossed that on the floor as well.

"Matching blouse with puffy sleeves? I don't think so!"

"A purple sweatshirt with pink hearts? Out of here!"

"Shorts with a cute kitty cat stitched onto the back

pocket. Forget it!"

Pretty soon, there was a large pile of clothes on Zibby's floor, and her closet was nearly empty. She was down to two pairs of jeans, some athletic shorts, a sweatshirt, and the T-shirt she was wearing.

She grabbed one of the pairs of jeans and studied them. "Cutesy embroidery on the tush? Nope. You're gone too." And she threw the jeans onto the heap.

But she still wasn't finished. She looked down at the shirt she was wearing – a baby blue T-shirt with a picture of two puppies. *How un-tomboy is that?* she thought to herself. So she ripped off the T-shirt, threw it on the pile and put on her pajama top – a neutral gray and white – which she felt most tomboys would approve of.

Then, as a final touch, she gathered all her shoes – except for her tennis shoes – and threw them onto the ground as well.

Satisfied, she slammed the closet door shut. She turned and looked at the pile on the floor. Then she was struck by another one of her Very Good Ideas. Her mom and dad were always telling her that she should help those in need. And Zibby herself loved to do good deeds. And here was one staring her right in the face.

She opened up her closet again and pulled out her suitcase and three old backpacks. One by one, she stuffed them full of her discarded clothes and shoes. She then lugged them down the stairs, and set them by the front door.

Her mother, hearing the clump, clump, clump of the luggage hitting the stairs, hurried into the entry hall from the kitchen.

"What's going on?" she asked, her eyes narrowing suspiciously.

"I've cleaned out my closet, and I'm donating all these clothes to the homeless. Isn't that great?" Zibby asked, feeling very proud of herself and her thoughtfulness. "I'm helping others, just like you've always taught us."

"Exactly *which* clothes are you donating?" her mom asked.

"All of them," Zibby exclaimed. "I have too many, and so many kids out there have none. Besides, I hate all these clothes. I'm never going to wear them anyway."

Her mom unzipped one of the backpacks and looked inside. Her lips tightened into a narrow line as they did whenever she became angry.

"Elizabeth Mildred Payne," she said sternly. "A lot of these clothes are brand new. You told me you just had to have them. How can you hate them?"

"I've changed, Mom," Zibby said matter-of-factly. "I'm a tomboy now. And tomboys don't wear these types of clothes. So I'm getting rid of them all."

"What do you mean you're a tomboy?" her mom asked, looking cross *and* confused. "When did this happen?"

"Earlier today," Zibby answered impatiently. "I've decided to play soccer with the boys at recess, so from now on, I'm only going to wear boy-ish clothes." She really didn't feel like wasting time filling her mom in on a decision that, to her, already felt like ancient history. She just wanted her mom to help her finish her good deed.

"Hey, can we take these down to the Salvation Army right now?" she asked.

"No," her mom replied, rubbing her temples. "We are not taking those clothes anywhere. But I think the bigger issue is, why are you suddenly a tomboy?"

She gave Zibby a penetrating look, and as she did, Zibby could feel her mom's anger turning into concern.

"Honey," her mom said in a softer voice, "is everything all right at school – with Sarah and the rest of your friends?"

Zibby rolled her eyes. Every time she made a change, her mom thought something was wrong, but nothing ever was.

"Everything is fine!" she said, a bit louder than she meant to.

"Okay, Zibby," her mom said. "Please calm down. I don't really know what's going on or why you suddenly want to turn into a tomboy, but if you want to, that's fine. However, you are not giving all your clothes away. Do you hear me?"

"I'll never wear them," she protested.

"You say that today, but in a week or a month you may change your mind," her mom said firmly. "For now, I'm putting these in my room." She grabbed two of the backpacks in one hand, slung another on her back, and grabbed the suitcase in the other hand.

"But I will *not* change my mind!" said Zibby. Didn't her mom know that when she made up her mind, that's how it stayed – forever?

As her mom struggled up the stairs with her load, she called to Zibby, "I wish I could fit into these clothes. I'd be lucky to have them hanging in my closet."

From upstairs, Zibby heard a door slam, and then there was silence.

Zibby still didn't understand what her mother was so worked up about. She should thank Zibby for wanting to help, not get mad! And her mother totally didn't get the tomboy thing. She seemed to think it was a problem – when it was actually *solving* all Zibby's problems.

"Nothing's going the way I thought it would this year," Zibby said grumpily to herself.

"When did life get so complicated?"

CHAPTER 7

THE DIFFERENCE BETWEEN BOYS AND GIRLS

"Uh-oh," Zibby said to herself the next morning as she got out of bed and started to change out of her pajamas and into her school clothes.

She'd done such a good job cleaning out her closet that she didn't even have one shirt to wear for school. What was she going to do?

But as soon as she'd asked herself the question, she'd already figured out the answer. Because right across the hall was an almost endless supply of clothes that were just right for tomboys. She ran across the hall and into Anthony's room. He was still sleeping, his covers twisted around his head.

She was nervous about waking him up; but on the other hand, he had to get up for school anyway. She shook him gently and whispered, "Anthony?"

"Get away," he mumbled, and rolled over.

"But I have to ask you something – can I borrow one of your shirts?"

"No."

"Why not?" Zibby asked.

"You've got your own clothes. Now get out of here!"

"But I don't like them anymore," she said pleadingly. "Just one, please."

"No, now scram!" he yelled, pulling the covers over his head.

Zibby couldn't believe how grumpy Anthony was being. It wasn't her fault he was sleeping in when he needed to get up – waking him up was actually a favor. And normally he was super sweet to her, and he always tried to help her out. *It must be Ashley*, she thought. *He's so wrapped up in her he doesn't even care about his little sister anymore.*

Zibby had figured his relationship with Ashley would be over by now, but it wasn't. Ashley and Anthony talked several times a day on the phone and, according to Zibby's mom, had met for yet another smoothie date.

Zibby wracked her brain for a way to persuade this new, unhelpful Anthony to come to her rescue. After a moment, she decided that good old-fashioned bribery might do the trick.

"If you let me wear one of your shirts," she bargained, "I'll water the lawn *and* take out the trash for you this week."

"No," came the muffled response.

"Oh come on, Anthony! Just let me have a shirt to wear and you don't have to do your chores."

The lump under the covers was silent.

"All right." Anthony's head popped up. "You can wear the basketball one if you want. In my top drawer. It's too small for me anyway."

"Thank you, thank you, thank you!" cried Zibby. She dug into his drawer, grabbed the faded blue T with an orange basketball on it, and then ran back to her room.

She pulled the T-shirt on and looked at herself in the full-length mirror on the back of her door. The shirt was a little baggy, but not too bad, even though the sleeves fell almost down to her elbows. She put on her shorts, pulled her hair back into a ponytail, slipped on her tennies, and was ready to go.

I'm ready for tomboy action, she thought to herself.

* * *

When Zibby walked onto the blacktop at school, Sarah, Amber, and Camille were already there. Sarah's eyes widened when she saw Zibby. Amber and Camille looked at each other and raised their eyebrows.

"*What* are you wearing?" asked Amber.

Zibby shrugged. "A T-shirt."

"Isn't that Anthony's shirt?" Sarah asked.

"Yep," said Zibby.

"*Why* are you wearing that?" asked Camille, with a look of disgust on her face.

Before Zibby could answer, Sarah explained, "Zibby's officially a tomboy now. And that means she dresses like a boy."

"That's right," nodded Zibby. "I am a tomboy." She threw her arms out to her sides like an actress taking a bow. "Ta da!"

She was about to tell Amber and Camille more about her Big Decision – even if they didn't seem to approve – when Matthew walked by and tapped her arm.

"Room Six versus Room Seven today at recess," said Matthew. "We need you today – we have to beat Room Seven – so be there!"

"You bet I will!" she said to Matthew, then thought excitedly, *I've chosen the perfect day to start being a total tomboy*.

Zibby left her friends and walked with Matthew. They talked about the game all the way back to class.

The game, however, wasn't as much fun as she'd thought it would be. Room Seven had several of the best soccer players in the school, and their team quickly scored three goals in a row, and was up 3–0. Matthew had an open shot, but missed, and Zane collided with another player, hurt his knee, and had to sit out for the rest of the game.

"We're never going to win," Matthew muttered under his breath to Zibby as they lined up for a play.

"Don't give up yet," she said, still hopeful.

And she was right to hope. In the second half of the game, the momentum switched, and Room Six scored two goals. Now the team was only down by one. Matthew called a "time out," and Zibby huddled close with her teammates.

"We only have a few more minutes," said Matthew. "We may not be able to win, but at least we can tie. If anyone gets near our goal, take the shot. We've got to get as many shots on goal as possible."

Zibby ran back into position, eager to help her team. She really wanted to be the one who scored a goal and tied the game. And that's why, when the ball rolled toward her and Matthew, in her excitement, she stepped in front of him, stole the ball away, and charged down toward her team's goal.

"I'm going to score! I know I'm going to score," she was saying to herself – just when a big kid from Room Seven blocked her, and kicked the ball from under her foot. He kicked it so hard that it went all the way down the field and landed in Room Seven's goal.

"Oh no!" Zibby covered her face.

"Oh no," the boys in her class groaned.

Just then, the bell rang. Room Seven had won the game 4–2.

Matthew stormed up to Zibby. "Nice move, tomboy! You stole the ball from me. I could have scored! You blew the game for us."

"I just wanted to help the team," she said.

"Next time, do your team a favor and *don't*!" he yelled.

His face was all red, and it almost looked as if he was crying. Zibby felt like crying herself. *Maybe I can't hack it on the field with the boys*, she thought. *Maybe this tomboy thing is a mistake. Maybe I should be back on the benches with Sarah and my other friends.*

Where were they, anyway? She looked around, but they were nowhere to be found. They must have gone back to class already.

Zibby walked back to class all alone.

To make matters worse, after recess they had English, and today they were learning how to distinguish between predicate nominatives, indirect objects, and direct objects. While Zibby liked writing essays, she hated learning about grammar, which she could never keep straight. She rolled her eyes and glanced around the classroom. In doing so, she met Matthew's eyes. He glared at her, and she looked away. But then she looked back and mouthed, "I'm sorry."

He continued to glare at her. She figured she'd try to apologize one more time.

"I won't do it again," she mouthed.

His eyes softened, and he shrugged his shoulders slightly. Zibby wasn't sure if she'd been forgiven, but she hoped so. A few minutes later, Matthew stopped by her desk during class discussion time, when the students were allowed to walk around and work together on projects.

"Need help, tomboy?" he asked.

"Yes. I hate all these stupid grammar terms," she exclaimed. "But you probably don't want to help me after the game."

"It's okay," he waved his hand. "You apologized."

"Really?" she asked. "I *am* super sorry."

"I know," he said. "Now let's look at these sentences together." He kneeled down by her desk.

Zibby couldn't believe her ears. When Sarah got mad at her, she sometimes wouldn't speak to Zibby for days. Once, when Zibby told Sarah her new jacket looked like dead hamster fur, Sarah didn't talk to her for a week. "But I like hamsters," Zibby had protested. "I think they're really cute!"

Zibby tried to concentrate on what Matthew was saying, but instead she was in the middle of a Big Revelation.

Boys don't stay mad the way girls do. They forget about it and move on.

She started to smile. *Wow*, she thought to herself. *This tomboy thing is getting better and better. I've got to keep it going.* Cleaning out her closet and wearing Anthony's shirt had been a great first step. And for sure, she'd ask Anthony for more shirts. But after that, what would her next tomboy move be?

CHAPTER 8

ZIBBY SAYS NO

A few days later, Zibby was sitting on her bed practicing what she'd decided was her Next Great Tomboy Skill – burping out the ABCs. Most of the sixth-grade boys did it, and Matthew could even make it all the way to "K." Zibby figured that with a little practice, she could belch as well as the boys.

So far, she had extended her burp to the letter "D." But she knew she was capable of more. She gulped in a big breath of air, swallowed, held her breath, then burped "A-B-C-D-E" before the burp gave out.

"Wow, I made it to another letter," she said to herself. "Excellent."

She was midway through another burp when she heard something coming from Anthony's room. Something high-pitched and feminine.

Zibby jumped out of her bed, scooted out the door, and tiptoed up to Anthony's door, which was closed. She leaned her ear on the door, trying to hear more, when suddenly the door opened. She almost fell over and onto a short girl with blonde hair, who was wearing a polo shirt and jeans.

"Ashley?" she asked, straightening herself up.

"Hi. You must be Zibby," Ashley smiled.

Zibby was in too much shock to smile back. *Anthony had Ashley in his room*, she thought to herself with alarm. *Alone. What is he thinking? What is my mother thinking?*

She probably would have stood there a lot longer, too surprised to move, but Anthony frowned at her and asked, "What are you doing right outside my door?" Then before she could answer, he added in a mean voice, "Scram!"

And Zibby did. She turned her back on them and ran downstairs as fast as she could.

"Mom," she called out, finding her mom in the kitchen playing "Go Fish" with Sam. "Ashley's in Anthony's room," she exclaimed. "Do something!"

Her mom smiled calmly. "They just ran up there to get some money. They're going out to get ice cream."

"I can't believe you let him have Ashley in there – and with the door shut!" Zibby said. She lowered her voice to a whisper. "They might kiss or something – gross!"

"I don't think they have time to do anything like that," her mom said reassuringly.

Their conversation was interrupted by the arrival of Anthony and Ashley. Zibby gave them the evil eye.

"Be back in a while," said Anthony gruffly, not looking at his mom or Zibby.

"Goodbye, Mrs. Payne. Bye, Zibby," Ashley said with a smile, as the two walked out of the room.

"She seems like a nice girl," said Zibby's mom.

Zibby rolled her eyes. *I don't care how nice she is*, she thought, irritated. *Ever since she came into Anthony's life, he's been acting like a jerk.* She sat there stewing until her mom said, "Since you're down here now, there's something I need to ask you." She put the cards down and turned on a TV show for Sam on the small kitchen TV on the counter. "But it's about a sensitive subject."

"What?" Zibby was immediately suspicious.

"Grandma Betty's birthday is coming up," her mom continued, "and she wants to take us all to The Oaks to celebrate. You know – that really nice restaurant where they put umbrellas in the drinks."

"I love it there," said Zibby. "Can I have a Shirley Temple with extra cherries?"

"Sure," said her mom with a smile. "Now, what I need to remind you of is that The Oaks is a fancy restaurant. You'll have to wear something nice."

"You mean the restaurant doesn't serve tomboys?" Zibby asked, wrinkling her brow.

Her mom's lips started to compress. "They serve tomboys. You just can't dress like one. For one night, you'll need to wear a skirt, a dress, or some nice pants."

"A restaurant can't *make* you wear something. It's a free country," Zibby exclaimed.

"Actually this restaurant does have a dress code it expects people to follow," her mom said. "And Zibby, I know that it would really make your grandmother happy if you wore that pretty dress she gave you for your birthday."

"The frilly one with all the bows on it? Forget it!" said Zibby. "Besides, I gave it away."

"Not officially," her mom reminded her. "All your clothes are still in my room. We just have to dig the dress out."

"No way!" Zibby yelled.

"Please stop yelling, Zibby," her mom said, her hands fluttering near her forehead as she began one of her Temple Rubs.

"Sorry, but when I feel strongly about things, I get loud. And I feel strongly that I should not have to wear a stupid dress to a restaurant."

"It's not just the restaurant, honey," her mom said. "It's about making your grandmother happy."

"But doesn't Grandma want to make *me* happy?" asked Zibby. "I'm a tomboy. Tomboys don't wear dresses."

"I understand," her mom said, sounding worn out. "But can't you make an exception this one time?"

"No." Zibby leapt up. "I won't. I won't do something I don't believe in!"

Her mom stood up as well. "I'll tell you what I believe in – showing respect for your mother and grandmother." She then grabbed the remote control and practically squeezed it to death turning off the TV. "Come on Sam, let's go upstairs – time for a bath."

Zibby couldn't believe how upset her mom was getting – again. She'd always told Zibby to stand up for herself. Well, she was. What did wearing a dress have to do with respect anyway? Her grandmother wouldn't care. Grandma Betty never wore dresses; she'd been wearing the same lime green pantsuit to every event since Zibby could remember.

What Zibby needed right now was some fresh air. She walked outside to the backyard to kick around the soccer ball. She'd only been playing for a few minutes when a voice behind her said, "Need another player?"

It was her dad, who was home early from work.

"Sure, Dad," she said enthusiastically. Her dad worked long hours and she didn't get to spend a lot of time with him. Maybe because of that, anything she did with him was special.

Only once they started kicking the ball back and forth, it seemed as if he wanted to talk more than he wanted to play soccer.

"Your mom tells me you won't wear a dress to Grandma Betty's dinner," he said.

Zibby suddenly stood still. "Is that why you wanted

to play soccer? To talk to me about that stupid dress?"

"No," her father cleared his throat. "I'm out here because I want to play soccer with my daughter. But I just thought since you and I are out here on our own, we could talk things over – like about what it means to be a tomboy."

"I know what it means," said Zibby, feeling insulted that her dad would think she'd become something without knowing what it was.

"Do you?" he asked. "Is it just about wearing boys' clothes and playing soccer?"

"Yes, that is exactly what it is," she responded. She knew her dad was fishing around for something else, but she was determined not to give it to him.

"Well, I think being a tomboy is more," he said. "I think it means being kind and respectful. And flexible. Do you know what I mean?"

"Of course," she dribbled the ball around her dad. "Flexible – like being able to touch your toes!" She smiled ruefully at her dad. "Just joking."

"Okay, then. So I think you, as a tomboy, need to go with the flow a bit more. Do some things that people who care about you ask you to do, even if you don't want to. That's my definition of a tomboy."

"And just where did you get this definition?" Zibby asked, feeling annoyed that her dad was preaching to her.

"The Payne Dictionary of Common Sense and

Decency."

"Yeah, right," Zibby said as she kicked the ball with all her might at the back fence. "That's not a real dictionary."

"Well, it should be, don't you think?"

She looked at her dad, and he smiled at her – one of his best "I love you even when you're being a pest" smiles that was impossible to resist.

Zibby sighed. "I'll think about what you said, okay? Now are we going to stand around all night yakking or are we going to play some soccer?"

"Let's play soccer," he replied, then ran to find the ball.

My dad is so easy to get along with, thought Zibby. *If only everyone were that way.* Because if her mom's reaction was any indication, becoming a tomboy and making tomboy stands was not going to go over well with everyone, no matter how much Zibby wanted it to.

CHAPTER 9

THE GIRLS GET GIGGLY

A few days later at breakfast, Zibby sat down between Anthony and Sam with her bowl of cereal. As she was taking her last bite, she felt a funny, hot sensation in her chest. She opened her mouth, and before she knew what had happened, out came a burp.

"Elizabeth Mildred Payne," her mother said crossly. "We do not burp at the table."

"Sorry," she said, not taking her mom's comment too seriously since Anthony had been burping at the table for years. In fact, she thought Anthony might speak up on her behalf, but instead he shot her an annoyed look and said, "Disgusting."

I should have known, she thought. *Now that he has a girlfriend, he's way too mature for burping.*

Sam, on the other hand, thought it was hysterical. He started saying "burp, burp, burp" over and over again, laughing like a maniac.

"See what you've done?" asked her mom, her mouth becoming a thin line.

"I didn't mean to," Zibby protested, wondering if

perhaps she shouldn't have practiced burping quite so much the other day.

As she was gathering her books and notebook to take to school, she remembered something else she'd been meaning to do for a while: return all of Sarah's shoes that were in the hall closet. She still had several miscellaneous lone shoes left over from shoe swapping during the summer. She gathered them up, and then threw them in a plastic garbage bag she found under the sink.

When she arrived at school, Amber, Camille and Sarah were already standing on the blacktop. Sarah was immediately curious about what Zibby was holding.

"What's in the bag?" she asked.

"Your shoes," said Zibby. "Since we're not swapping anymore, I thought you'd want these back. Now you'll have complete sets again."

"Oh," said Sarah, not looking as happy to get the shoes back as Zibby had thought she would. "Are you sure you don't want to hold on to them for a while?" she asked. "You never know. You might change your mind. And then you, me, and Camille could have a three-way swap."

Zibby was flattered that Sarah still wanted to include her, but on the other hand, she didn't want to give her false hope. "Umm, I'm not going to be changing my mind. I mean, come on." She dug around in the sack and pulled out a sandal with a pink butterfly on the strap. "No tomboy would be caught dead in this."

Sarah snatched the shoe out of her hand and threw it back in the bag.

"You know what, Zibby?" she said. "You can be a real pain. I guess that's where you got your name!" She turned her back on Zibby and faced Amber and Camille.

"Hey wait a minute, Sarah, I ..." Zibby started to say, when she felt the pressure building up in her chest – and a second later, she let out a large burp.

"That is so totally gross," said Sarah, whipping around. Amber and Camille wrinkled up their noses like they were going to be sick.

"Well, Zibby, I guess you really *are* a tomboy," Amber said disdainfully.

"And what's wrong with that?" asked Zibby.

Amber looked at Sarah and Camille. The three girls shared a knowing smile, then walked off to class without even saying goodbye.

How rude, thought Zibby.

What is Sarah so upset about, anyway? she wondered. So maybe she'd come on a little too strong about not wanting to wear Sarah's shoes anymore, but was it her fault that tomboys don't wear sandals with butterflies on them? And maybe she shouldn't have burped, but could she help it that burps had suddenly started coming out of her mouth without her even wanting them to?

Maybe if Sarah understood this, she wouldn't be so mad, she thought. Zibby tried to catch Sarah's eye all morning in class, hoping they could meet in the bathroom to talk, but Sarah wouldn't look at her.

During recess later that day, she thought that hanging out with Sarah, Amber and Camille might be a good peace offering, but instead of sitting down on the benches, the girls went out to the far end of the soccer field. They stood there, holding hands and giggling as if they were in on some big private joke.

Zibby walked over to them. "What's so funny?" she asked.

"Nothing," they replied in unison.

"And even if we are laughing, it has nothing to do with you," said Sarah.

"Who does it have to do with then?" Zibby asked.

"Someone else," said Sarah.

"Yeah, someone else," repeated Amber, and she giggled again.

"Like who?" Zibby asked.

The three girls looked at each other. Then Camille said in a whisper, "Like someone whose name begins with 'M'."

An "M"? What were they talking about? Zibby looked out on the field. The only person whose name started with an "M" was Matthew.

"You mean Matthew?" she asked.

At the mention of his name, the three girls said "Shhh" and looked around as if to make sure no one was looking. Then they burst into more giggles.

"You guys are crazy," Zibby said, before running out to the field to play soccer. During the entire game, the girls stood on the sidelines, giggling as if watching soccer was the funniest thing to ever happen to them in their lives. They did the same thing during afternoon recess as well.

After school ended that day, Zibby fell in step with Sarah as she was leaving the classroom, in order to ask her what was going on during recess. But Sarah had forgotten her math book, and had to run back to class to retrieve it. As Zibby was waiting for Sarah, Amber walked by, so Zibby asked her instead.

"What was so funny out on the soccer field?"

"Nothing," said Amber coldly.

"Tell me," said Zibby.

Amber looked around as if to make sure no one was listening.

"It's just that he's so cute! Mega-cute!"

"Who?" asked Zibby.

"Matthew!" Amber squealed.

"Cute?" Zibby exploded. "Matthew? We've known him since kindergarten. He's not cute. He's a friend!"

Zibby couldn't believe it. It was bad enough that Amber and Camille were always talking about which TV star or singer was cute, and now they were talking about the sixth-grade boys in the same way.

Suddenly Sarah was standing on the other side of Zibby. She must have been listening in on the conversation because she whispered, "For your information, Matthew is very cute and a lot of girls think so. But you wouldn't notice because you're a tomboy. And tomboys just see boys as friends. But we don't. We see them as more."

"Since when?"

"Since all year," said Sarah, linking her arm through Amber's and speeding up, leaving Zibby behind.

That's the stupidest thing I've ever heard, she thought. *They're acting like love-struck teenagers or something.*

She stomped the rest of the way home. When she got to the corner of her street, she saw Anthony and Ashley, already home from high school, leaning against a tree and talking. And they were holding hands! She couldn't help but stare. When Ashley and Anthony noticed her looking at them, they quickly dropped hands. Ashley gave her a little wave, and Anthony stared at his feet.

"A public display of affection," Zibby said to herself in disgust. "Gross."

She knew that to be polite she should wave back at Ashley, but she felt too uncomfortable to pretend everything was normal. Instead, she looked down at the sidewalk and walked past them as quickly as she could.

When she got to her house, she ran to the front door and up the stairs to her room.

Once inside, she turned on the Eagles full blast, trying to erase the day's events from her mind. *Things couldn't possibly get any weirder this year*, she thought to herself grumpily. And even the sound of one of her Favorite Bands on the Planet couldn't make her feel better.

CHAPTER 10

THE TOMBOY CLUB IS BORN

The next morning, Zibby burst into Anthony's room, hoping to borrow yet another shirt. He'd already given her several more since the first one, but they were all in the wash now. In his recent mood, she wasn't that hopeful he'd give her yet another one, but it was her only option. Besides, he had tons of shirts – his drawers were stuffed with them.

"No," he snapped from underneath his covers when she asked. "I'm not giving you any more. And quit waking me up!"

"But I'm out of shirts," she pleaded.

"I've hardly got any I like, and you've taken enough. Wear your own clothes!"

"Well, thanks a lot," she said. "I used to have a nice brother, but I guess he doesn't live here anymore." And she stormed out of his room.

She went downstairs, still in her PJs, and into the kitchen where her mom was feeding Sam Cheerios. She'd have to appeal to her mom for help – even though she wasn't being very supportive of Zibby's new taste in clothes.

"Mom, I *have* to have some new T-shirts."

Her mom's forehead creased. "Not that again, Zibby. You have new clothes. In the bags in my closet."

"But you know I can't wear them! I need some T-shirts. Some boy T-shirts."

"I am not buying you any more clothes," her mom said firmly. "You will have to find something to wear."

Her dad walked into the kitchen. "You can wear one of my shirts," he said. "Of course, it will be about ten times too big for you."

"I hope you're joking," her mom said to him. She then turned to Zibby. "Please get upstairs and find something to wear – *now* – and stop bothering us about buying you any more new clothes."

Zibby walked back up to her room, and threw open her closet where her dirty clothes hamper was. She grabbed the blue University of California T-shirt she'd worn yesterday ... and the day before. Okay, so it was a little bit dirty – the field had been muddy yesterday, and there were brown streaks on the back of the shirt – but it wasn't that bad! She turned it inside out and did the sniff check under the arms, and *wooh*, the shirt was a bit stinky. But once she put it on, and the shirt was right side out, it didn't smell ... much.

On the blacktop that morning, Amber and Camille shot her "a look."

"Didn't you already wear that shirt a few times this week?" asked Sarah, looking at Zibby worriedly.

"And don't get too close," cried Amber, holding her nose. "You stink, Zibby Payne!"

"I do not," she cried out. She'd never admit that she did – especially to Amber.

Zibby clomped toward class, feeling sorry for herself, when Matthew walked by and tapped her lightly on the shoulder. "See you on the field at recess," he smiled at her.

Zibby brightened. Maybe her girl friends didn't like her anymore, but at least the boys still did.

During class, Miss Cannon had a special announcement to make. "Today I'm assigning solar system reports. I want you to buddy up with one or two other students and choose a planet, the sun, or the moon to write about," she said in her monotone voice. "Raise your hand once you've found a partner. The final report will be due in two weeks."

How fun, thought Zibby. She and Sarah could choose the moon – their favorite "heavenly body." Over the summer, she and Sarah had spent hours watching it from the backyard, and had even written a song about how instead of being made of green cheese, it was made out of mint chip ice cream – their favorite flavor. But before she had time to raise her hand and suggest her plan to Miss Cannon, Sarah raised hers.

"Amber, Camille, and I will do the moon," she said.

Traitor! thought Zibby.

One by one, her classmates partnered up and chose their planets until only one planet was left. *Pluto – the absolute worst planet to write about because less is known about it than any other one*, thought Zibby, her heart sinking.

And there was only one kid left to do her report with – Drew Dinklesbuhl – who was a total drip. Plus, he never finished his assignments, so she knew she'd wind up doing most of the work.

At lunch, Zibby sat down alone at a table with her sandwich and apple. Even though there were a lot of empty tables to choose from, Sarah, Amber, and Camille sat down at the table directly in front of her and huddled together over a magazine. Zibby strained her eyes, trying to see what the magazine was. *Teenyboppers Forever.* A teen magazine. With BB5 on the cover.

And that's when it hit her – the Big Revelation that Sarah, Amber, and Camille had become their own group. Their own *club*. And she definitely was not in it.

And that's when another Big Revelation hit her. When your best friends form a club and don't include you, there's only one thing you can do. Form your own club. And don't include them.

And there was only one club she was interested in starting. The Tomboy Club. "That will show them," she said to herself. They'd see that she wasn't so weird, and that other girls were tomboys too. And that way, the next time she had to do a report in class, she'd have a friend to do it with. Someone who was a tomboy just like her.

The Tomboy Club will be the best club at the school – no – on the planet, she decided. There was only one little detail to work out, however. Who should she get to be in it?

CHAPTER 11

THE GREAT TOMBOY TRYOUTS

Zibby searched the lunch tables, looking for good tomboy material. Her eyes fell on Jasmine, who was a great athlete, and wore basketball shorts to school every day. But Jasmine was shy – she hardly ever said a word. And one thing Zibby thought tomboys had to do was talk. Very loudly. So Jasmine was out, Zibby decided.

Carmen, Jane, Lyla, and Courtney weren't right either. They were the class goody goodies – and in Zibby's opinion, another thing tomboys weren't was especially good. Monica and Amanda were out, too. They were total Amber wanna-bes ... every day their T-shirts got tighter and their skirts got shorter.

This might not be as easy as I hoped, thought Zibby.

"On the other hand, appearances can be deceiving," she said to herself. Just because a girl didn't seem like a tomboy on the outside didn't mean she wasn't one on the inside.

But how will I find out? And she was suddenly hit with the Absolute Best Idea. She'd hold tomboy try-outs! This way, girls who wanted to be tomboys would come to *her*.

She grabbed a piece of paper out of her notebook, and in fat purple Magic Marker wrote:

Calling All Tomboys for an Ultra-Exclusive Tomboy Club. If interested, meet Zibby Payne tomorrow in the bathroom during morning recess. Tomboys Unite!

She stuck the notice on the bathroom door where everyone was sure to see it.

At morning recess the next day, she hustled over to the bathroom, a notebook and clipboard in hand. She was disappointed to see that only four girls had shown up.

I guess tomboys aren't that popular these days, she said to herself. *Oh well, let's see what we've got here.*

One of the girls was named Bernice. Bernice had a unibrow, which was promising, as tomboys didn't care what their eyebrows looked like, Zibby decided. But she wore a skirt, which was not so promising.

At least it's not a short one, Zibby thought to herself.

"You first," said Zibby, pointing to Bernice. "Follow me." She led Bernice into one of the bathroom stalls and motioned her to sit on the closed lid of the toilet seat.

"I've written up a little quiz to test your tomboy worthiness," Zibby said. "Please answer the questions as honestly and completely as possible."

"Okay," Bernice nodded, looking a little nervous.

"Question Number One: What's your favorite lip gloss?" asked Zibby.

"I don't know," said Bernice thoughtfully. "Sometimes I borrow my brother's Blistex."

"Excellent answer," smiled Zibby. "Question Number Two: Boys – which ones at school do you think are cute?"

"Err, um ... none," said Bernice.

"Another excellent answer," Zibby nodded approvingly. "Question Number Three: Athletic ability. Rate it on a scale of good, okay, or plain-out terrible."

"Good," said Bernice.

"Awesome," smiled Zibby as she made a note. "And finally," she continued. "The fourth and last question. If your friends didn't want to play tetherball with you anymore, and instead wanted to sit around and put on makeup, fix hair, and talk about boys and act like total jerks and even make fun of you, *what would you do*?" She didn't mean to yell out this last part, but thinking about how her friends had been treating her, she just couldn't help it.

"You're yelling," said Bernice.

"Excuse me," said Zibby. "I'll try to speak more softly. So, *what would you do*?" she yelled.

"Um, err, I don't know," Bernice said tentatively. "Do what my friends wanted to do, I guess."

Zibby shot Bernice an icy look and crossed out her name in the notebook.

"Bernice, I'm sorry. You're just not right for the club.

Thank you for your time, though."

Bernice's face crumpled. "I never get picked for anything," she said huffily.

"Maybe next time you should try a less exclusive club," said Zibby, having no sympathy for Bernice after her last answer. She opened the door and let Bernice out of the stall.

"Next," she called out.

Three interviews later, all of which contained flawed answers, Zibby had to admit that there wasn't a tomboy among the girls. It looked as if her club might have to exist with only one member – herself. *But how fun would that be?*

"Maybe I should just forget the whole thing," she said to herself disappointedly, when someone came running through the bathroom door – Vanessa Heartgabel, the Absolute Weirdest Girl in Sixth Grade.

"Sorry I'm late. Can I still try out for the Tomboy Club?" she asked Zibby.

Zibby stared at her.

"Give me a minute, will you?" she went back into the bathroom stall and sat down on the toilet.

Vanessa Heartgabel wore the same plaid pants to school almost every day with an oversized black sweatshirt, no matter how hot it was. She usually wore her hair in three pigtails, except for the time she showed up with four. And even though she was eleven, she carried a Barney lunch pail. She didn't have any friends except for two fifth-grade girls who also wore their hair in multiple pigtails.

On the other hand, thought Zibby, *Vanessa is tough.* She'd been teased since first grade and it didn't seem to bother her. She was also strong – Zibby had once seen her go across the monkey bars eight times in a row without stopping – a class record. And Vanessa was loud – in last year's fifth grade safety play, she'd played the part of an ambulance. Her siren was so convincing, neighbors down the street came running to see where the accident was.

But the very best thing Vanessa had going for her was she was Zibby's last hope. It was Vanessa or no one.

Zibby emerged from the stall and addressed Vanessa. "I've decided that out of all the girls in the school, I am selecting you to be part of my Tomboy Club. And you don't even have to try out! You're in. Just like that. So do you want to join?"

"Okeydokey," said Vanessa. That was another weird thing about Vanessa. She said "okeydokey" a lot.

"Is that a yes?" asked Zibby.

"Yes," said Vanessa. "No one's ever asked me to be in a club before. Thanks, Zibby," she smiled. There was a blob of something brown between her two front teeth.

"No, thank *you*, Vanessa," Zibby replied. "I'll call you tonight to go over some details for tomorrow."

"Okeydokey," said Vanessa, flashing the brown-blob-between-her-two-front-teeth smile again, and scooted out the door.

Zibby smiled triumphantly. She had found someone after all. The Tomboy Club had begun.

Her spirits fell a little bit with her next thought, however. Because now she'd have to figure out something for the Tomboy Club to do!

CHAPTER 12

A HAIRCUT TO REMEMBER

That afternoon, Zibby sat on her bed making a list of some tomboy activities she and Vanessa could tackle together.

1. Play soccer at recess (of course).

2. Swap shorts (*if Vanessa has any – I'll have to find out if Vanessa has anything to wear besides those plaid pants*).

3. Perfect the alphabet burp.

"And what will number four be?" she asked herself. "It should be something dramatic. Something radical."

"I know!" She scribbled:

4. Get super-short boy haircuts.

Too bad she had to get a matching cut with the weirdest girl in sixth grade, but at this point, she couldn't afford to be picky.

She called Vanessa up, and discussed the list with her. Vanessa had one pair of athletic shorts, and she agreed to wear them tomorrow. She also said the soccer and burping "sounded okeydokey" to her, and that, during dinner that night, she'd ask her parents for

71

a haircut.

Her parents should be happy to agree, thought Zibby. *Any haircut is better than three ponytails!*

Zibby wandered into the kitchen where her dad was grabbing a drink out of the refrigerator. *Perfect timing*, thought Zibby. Here was her dad, all alone, and he was a lot easier to sell on new ideas than her mom – especially lately!

"Hi, Dad!" She gave him a big hug.

"Hi, Zibs. How was school today?"

"Great! I started a Tomboy Club."

Her dad looked amused. "And what exactly is a Tomboy Club?"

"A really cool, exclusive club at school where other girls – well, at least one other girl – and I get to do totally cool tomboy things," she said.

"Sounds fun," her dad said as he sat down at the kitchen table.

"It is," she said. "And one of the really fun things we want to do is get our hair cut really short, like boys. So do you think I could get my hair cut this weekend?"

"Hmm," her dad considered. "How short do you want it exactly?"

"This short." She touched the top part of her ear.

"That's awfully short," he said, looking doubtful.

"Well, if I don't like it, it will always grow," Zibby said sensibly.

"Good point," said her dad. "I don't know, though. You'd better ask your mom. She runs the show around here, you know."

"Okay, but put in a good word for me, would you Dad?" Zibby asked. "I think she's still mad at me about the dress, and – like I've told her a zillion times – there is no way on earth I'm wearing that to Grandma Betty's dinner!" She gave her dad another hug and ran back up to her room, where she flopped down on her bed and consulted her tomboy activity list again.

A few minutes later, her mom knocked on her door. "Can I come in?"

"Sure," Zibby replied.

"Dad told me about your new club and the haircut," she said in a soft, measured tone that Zibby recognized as her "I don't want to get into another fight" voice. "Now, I don't mind you cutting your hair, but if you cut it that short," she motioned to her ears with her hands, "it will take months to grow out if you don't like it. And honestly, Zibby, I don't think you'll like it."

"I will too," said Zibby, annoyed that her mom was challenging yet another one of her Very Good Ideas.

Her mom sat down on her bed and took a deep breath. "I know you're going through something right now. I know sixth grade isn't what you thought it would be. I know you're a tomboy now. But I also know that getting a short haircut won't make sixth grade better, and

I'm saying no. Your dad agrees. And that's final."

"You don't understand." Zibby jumped off the bed. "If I want to make the Tomboy Club really good, we have to do some big things. Take some risks. Otherwise, it will be a flop."

"I'm sure there is something else *big* you can do besides cut all your hair off," her mom countered. "Maybe Sarah could help you think of something."

"Sarah?" Zibby said, heatedly. "She's not in the club. I wouldn't ask her anything about being a tomboy."

"Oh," said her mom, looking confused. "I just figured Sarah was in it."

"We're hardly friends anymore, Mom," Zibby said, rolling her eyes. "At school she spends all her time with Amber and Camille, and I play soccer with the boys. She practically doesn't even talk to me."

"Oh," her mom said thoughtfully. "That must be hard. You must miss Sarah."

"I don't miss her," said Zibby, exasperated. "Why should I miss someone who doesn't even like me anymore? The only thing making me unhappy is that you won't let me cut my hair. You're wrecking everything!"

Her mom sighed, then said in her most patient tone of voice, "If Dad and I can't talk sense into you, maybe your brother can."

"Anthony? No way," exclaimed Zibby. "All he cares

about now is Ashley. *He* doesn't like me anymore either."

"He's just embarrassed," said her mom. "He doesn't know how to act around us when he's with Ashley. Or how to handle all the new feelings he's experiencing. It will take some time, but he'll learn."

"Right." Zibby rolled her eyes. *Just because Anthony has "new feelings" doesn't excuse his behavior*, she thought.

Her mom stood up. "Well, we can talk more about everything later. But in the meantime, no haircut, and my decision is final." She headed for the door. "I'd better go check on Sam – he's been quiet way too long. I hope he hasn't gotten into the permanent Magic Markers again."

After her mom left, Zibby sat there and fumed. Her mom was so unfair. She didn't understand anything about sixth grade.

Well, she'd show her! Zibby didn't need her mother's permission to cut her hair. She didn't have to go to any haircutting salon. She could do it herself.

Zibby marched into the bathroom and grabbed the small nail scissors. She stood in front of the mirror and held out a big handful of hair over the top of her left ear.

"There," she said, cutting off the piece. "The tomboy haircut begins."

But as soon as she'd made the cut, she was sorry. What had she done? Now, hanging above her ear, she had a big clump of short hair that was so ugly and uneven it looked as if Sam had hacked it off. It was as if someone had slapped a toupee on half her head – a really bad one that even the baldest man on the planet wouldn't want to wear.

"Why did I have to cut my own hair?" she asked herself, throwing the nail scissors onto the ground and starting to cry.

If Sarah were around, she'd know what to do, she thought. *Sarah's good at things like fixing hair. But Sarah isn't around anymore.* And with that last thought echoing in her head, she fled the bathroom and ran into her room, where she flung herself down on her bed and cried some more.

CHAPTER 13

THE TOMBOY CLUB FIZZLES

The next morning, Zibby woke up early, locked herself in the bathroom, and tried to fix her hair. She slicked the short pieces back with water so that they would blend in with the rest of her hair, but the hair was stubborn and wouldn't stay back. She then tried to feather her hair with the nail scissors as she'd seen a hairdresser once do to her mom, but it just made the pieces stick out more. She thought about clipping the pieces back with a barrette, but since tomboys don't wear barrettes, that *wasn't* an option.

Finally she decided just to let the hair be, no matter how bad it looked. *Who cares, anyway*, she thought. *Tomboys could give a rat's tail about what they look like!*

Zibby tried to sneak out of the house so her mom wouldn't see that she'd disobeyed her, but her hunger tripped her up. The cereal cabinet was right next to the hall closet. She tried to hide in the closet and reach across to grab the cereal box so she could eat a few handfuls for breakfast. But she couldn't quite get her hands on the box, and wound up tipping over and lurching into the cabinet – in plain view of her mom and Anthony, who were sitting at the nearby breakfast table.

"Your hair!" Her mom's eyes and mouth widened in shock. "What happened?"

"I had a little accident with the scissors, that's all," said Zibby, trying to be nonchalant despite the fact that her eyes were beginning to sting in that pre-cry way.

"I'd call that a *big* accident," Anthony said.

Zibby glared at him. At the same time, her mother was glaring at her.

"I clearly said you could not cut your hair, and you did it anyway," she said in an accusing voice.

Zibby was silent.

"Not only did you disobey me, now we'll have to pay a professional for a haircut to fix the damage," her mom said. "There are going to be consequences for this."

Zibby bit her lip to keep them from trembling, but under her mother's disapproving eye, the tears started to flow.

"Go ahead and punish me," she yelled. "I don't care." Then she ran back upstairs.

* * *

Alone in her room, she thought, *isn't my hair punishment enough*? She knew she'd done something stupid. Why did she need to suffer anymore?

Just then, there was a knock on her door. Before she could say "Go away," the door opened and Anthony appeared.

"What do *you* want?" she asked crossly.

"Hey kid." He came over and patted her on the arm. "Don't worry about Mom. She feels sorry for you, so she's not going to be too hard on you. I can tell. And as for your hair, I have the perfect solution."

He held out a brown beanie cap.

"Where'd you get that?"

"It's Ashley's – she left it here the other day. But I know she wouldn't mind if you wore it," he said. "It will totally hide your haircut, plus, all your friends will think it's cool because this style of hat is really in at the high school."

Zibby reached out and took the hat. She placed it on her head and pulled it down tightly.

Hmm, she thought. *It looks pretty good. You can't even see the haircut.*

She turned to her brother.

"Thanks," she said, thinking, *I guess he can still be nice sometimes.*

Now that her hair problem was solved, she began to cheer up. *Time to get on with the Tomboy Club*, she thought. She grabbed her things and headed out the door.

At school, Vanessa came running up to her on the blacktop.

"My mom said I can't cut my hair!" she exclaimed.

"It's probably a good idea if you don't," said Zibby dryly, then added, "so don't worry about it. We can still switch shorts at first recess, okay?"

"Okeydokey," said Vanessa, swinging her Barney lunch pail.

During morning recess, Zibby and Vanessa went into side-by-side bathroom stalls.

"One, two, three, take off your shorts," Zibby called out. "Now hand them under." The girls handed each other their shorts underneath the stalls.

"One, two, three, put the other pair on!" commanded Zibby. She pulled up Vanessa's shorts, but the waistband was so big, they fell below her hips. Meanwhile, she could hear Vanessa grunting in the stall next to her.

"I ... can't ... fit ... into ... these!" she gasped.

"Let's see." Zibby crawled under the divider and into Vanessa's stall. Zibby's shorts were stuck at Vanessa's thighs, and Vanessa's long, loose T-shirt hung down to meet them.

"This is as far as I can pull them up!" huffed Vanessa.

I should have known, thought Zibby. *Vanessa is way bigger than I am.*

"It's okay, Vanessa," she said. "Tomboys don't have to switch shorts. It just sounded fun. We can still practice burping at lunch and play soccer with the boys during afternoon recess."

Vanessa was so weird that Zibby figured she'd be a natural at burping. But when they sat down at the lunch tables and she showed Vanessa how to swallow, hold her breath, and let out a burp, Vanessa couldn't do it.

"It hurts," she whimpered. "All that swallowing is giving me a stomachache."

"Wait a minute," said Zibby. "I know what to do." She ran over to the soda machine, unearthed a dollar from her pocket, and bought a soda. Then she rushed back to Vanessa.

"Drink a few sips quickly, then hold your breath and swallow," she commanded.

Vanessa did as she was told. But instead of burping, some of the soda came back up her throat and she spit it up over her shirt.

"Gross!" said Zibby.

"This is absolutely not okeydokey," said Vanessa. "I hate burping!"

"Okay, okay," said Zibby. "Don't worry. It's not a big deal. Tomboys don't have to burp. We can still play soccer with the boys next recess."

When afternoon recess arrived, Zibby grabbed Vanessa's arm and went running with her out to the soccer field.

"Matthew, you know Vanessa. She's a tomboy too, and today she's playing with us."

Matthew looked skeptical. "All right," he said. "But she's not on my team."

When the game started, Zibby was surprised that Vanessa didn't move. She stood in the middle of the field like a statue.

Oh no, thought Zibby, wondering for the first time if maybe Vanessa couldn't play soccer.

As Vanessa stood there, frozen, the ball came rolling by her. From both sides, the boys rushed to the ball. Vanessa put her hands up to her face in terror. The next thing Zibby knew, Vanessa was lying on the ground, crying and screaming about a skinned knee.

The boys gathered around her. Zibby came running up as well.

"The boys trampled all over me," Vanessa screamed. "I'm bleeding!"

"You were in our way," said Matthew apologetically. "We didn't mean to hurt you."

"Can I help?" Zibby held her hand out to Vanessa to help her up. Vanessa pushed Zibby's hand away.

"No, you cannot help, Zibby Payne," yelled Vanessa, standing up on her own. "My stomach hurts from lunch. My knee hurts from soccer. And you know what else? I quit the Tomboy Club!"

She ran off the field sniffing loudly.

Zibby sighed. So that was it. The whole Tomboy Club had gone down the drain.

"Oh, so what?" she said to herself as she kicked the ground. It was a stupid idea anyway. She was the only true tomboy in the entire school. There was no way a club would ever work.

Zibby stomped off the field. She didn't feel like playing anymore today either. Instead, she wandered off toward the benches. As she got closer to them, she saw Sarah sitting all alone – for once, she wasn't surrounded by Amber and Camille. Zibby walked slowly over to her.

"Hi," she said cautiously, not knowing how Sarah would respond. She was relieved when Sarah smiled back and said, "Hi."

"Nice hat," Sarah continued.

Zibby's hand instinctively jerked up and touched the beanie.

"Um, thanks," she said.

"No soccer today?" asked Sarah.

"Long story," said Zibby.

"Try me," said Sarah.

"Well," Zibby took a deep breath, "I started a Tomboy Club, and invited Vanessa to join, but turns out she hates soccer, and she fell down and got hurt, and it was all such a mess I just quit playing for the day."

"Oh. I'm sorry," said Sarah.

Zibby wasn't sure if Sarah was really sorry or was just saying it, but it felt good to be talking again to Sarah, so she decided to tell her more.

"Vanessa already quit the Tomboy Club – after just one day," said Zibby. "And now I don't have a club to belong to anymore."

"Why do you need to belong to a club?" asked Sarah, looking confused.

"Because everyone else is in one," Zibby replied a little hotly.

"Who's 'everyone'?" asked Sarah.

"You, Amber, and Camille, that's who," replied Zibby. "You're in the FOAAC Club."

"The what?" Sarah asked, squinting her eyes and crinkling up her nose.

"The Friends of Amber and Camille club."

"That's not a club!"

"It feels like one to me." Zibby hung her head down. "And it's a club I'm definitely not invited into."

"Well, you *did* start a club – and didn't invite me," replied Sarah. "And before that, you ditched me for the boys. It's like all you care about is soccer – forget your friends!"

"That's not true," exclaimed Zibby. "I never wanted to forget you!"

Sarah looked at her doubtfully. But then her eyes softened, and she smiled. She was about to say something when suddenly Amber and Camille appeared and sat down on either side of her.

Amber hugged Sarah and so did Camille. Then

Amber looked over at Zibby and snippily said, "Hi."

"Hi back," said Zibby, trying to sound nonchalant.

"Time to go, girls," said Amber, standing up, and pulling Sarah and Camille up with her. "After school we can go to my house, where that new BB5 CD is just waiting for us."

She linked arms with Sarah on one side and Camille on the other, and the three girls started to walk away. After they'd taken a few steps, Sarah turned back and mouthed a "Bye" to Zibby.

Zibby put up her hand and gave a wave, then Sarah turned back around and started laughing at something Camille was saying.

Zibby thought about following Sarah, pulling her away from Amber and Camille, and linking her own arm with Sarah's as they used to do. But what if Sarah didn't want to walk with her anymore? It would be too humiliating – especially after everything that had happened that day. So instead, she just watched as her best friend ... her former best friend... walked away. Zibby looked – and felt – like one very lonely tomboy.

CHAPTER 14

IF THE SHOE FITS

After school that day, Zibby didn't practice burping. She didn't ask Anthony for more shirts. She didn't write any more tomboy activity lists. She came home and threw herself on the living room couch, then grabbed one of the sofa throws and pulled it all the way up and over her head.

"Of all the bad days I've had this year, this day was the absolute worst," she said to herself. "I think I'll just hide here forever. Sixth grade can go on without me."

Her privacy, however, was shattered when someone abruptly ripped the blanket off her head. It was Sam, smiling at her. And her mom was right behind him.

"What are you doing, Zibby?" her mom asked with a concerned look.

"Nothing – just relaxing," she said curtly. The day had been such a disaster, she couldn't even begin to tell someone about it – especially her mom! She glared at her brother and mother, hoping they'd get the hint and leave her alone.

"Sam, why don't you finish up your coloring in the

kitchen." Zibby's mom started to lead him out of the room. "And Zibby, I'll be right back."

If she asks me what's wrong, I'm not telling her one thing, thought Zibby stubbornly. But when her mom returned and sat on the edge of the sofa, Zibby surprised herself by blurting out, "This whole tomboy thing has been terrible. I thought it would be fun because I could play soccer and run around with the boys at recess, instead of doing dopey things like fix hair and do nails with Sarah, but nothing has worked out the way I wanted it to. I don't have any friends. I've lost Sarah. And Amber and Camille hate me."

"Hate you? That's a pretty strong word," her mom said. "And I'm sure you haven't lost Sarah for good."

"Yes I have, Mom, and it's all her fault. She's trying to be so grown up and it's wrecked everything. She thinks I'm just a stupid, smelly tomboy."

Her mom was silent for a moment. Then, very gently, she asked, "Is Sarah the only one who's changed? You've changed a lot too, you know."

"So?" asked Zibby, not understanding what her mom was getting at.

"Well," her mom said carefully, "if your feelings are hurt because Sarah doesn't want to spend time with you anymore, is it possible that *her* feelings are hurt because you quit spending recess with her?"

"No," Zibby started to say, then thought about it.

Hmm, maybe she has a point. What had Sarah said today – that Zibby had "ditched" her for the boys?

"And just maybe," her mom continued, seemingly encouraged because Zibby hadn't tried to argue, "if you made a little effort toward Sarah, she'd do the same with you. And once you patch it up with her, I bet the rest of your friends will come around too."

Zibby stared at her mom. She and her mom didn't always see eye to eye, but she had to admit, her mom was pretty wise when it came to friends.

"You really think things can get better?"

"I definitely do," her mom smiled.

"Thanks, Mom," she smiled back, throwing off the blanket and jumping off the couch.

"Oh, and I almost forgot." Her mom stood up, reaching into her back pocket. "I bought you something today at the drug store." She handed Zibby a plain white cotton headband.

Zibby looked confused.

"To hide your haircut," her mom explained. "After all, you can't wear that beanie cap forever. If you push all your hair back in the headband, I don't think you'll be able to see how uneven the front is."

"Thanks," said Zibby.

"And one more thing," said her mom. "Your punishment for disobeying will be extra chores around the house, so that you can pay for a decent haircut to fix the one you gave yourself. Okay?"

"Okay," nodded Zibby.

She walked slowly up to her room, still thinking about the conversation she'd had with her mom. Maybe she *was* partly to blame for her split with Sarah. Because, even though it seemed as if Sarah and her other friends had been trying to turn into teenagers overnight, Zibby had been trying just as hard to change into an instant tomboy. And maybe that wasn't the smartest thing to do either. Maybe no one could really change that much, that quickly – or at least, not that easily.

She thought back to the evening when she and her dad played soccer in the backyard. What was it he had said? That tomboys needed to be "flexible." Well, maybe she hadn't been as "flexible" as she could have been. Because even if she did hate some of the things the girls did at recess, she didn't hate Amber or Camille – no matter how dopey they'd been acting lately – and she certainly didn't hate Sarah. Sarah was her best friend. So maybe she should try harder to do at least some of the things Sarah liked.

And then, she was struck with another one of her Very Good Ideas.

She grabbed a piece of paper from her notebook, and on it, wrote:

Dear Sarah: Do you think we could start a new club?
A Zibby and Sarah club?

Love, Zibby

PS: I'm sorry about the shoes.

PPS: I'm sorry about the recesses.

PPPS: I'm sorry about the entire sixth-grade year so far.

She tore out the page, folded it, and wrote "Sarah" on the top. She ran out of her house and all the way to Sarah's. Once she was there, she rang the doorbell, and quickly slipped the note under the door.

Zibby turned and ran home, not stopping until she was back in her room. She hoped Sarah would say yes to her idea. But even if she didn't, at least Zibby had tried to fix their friendship. For once, the tomboy had been flexible.

She hadn't been back home for more than fifteen minutes when the doorbell rang. She ran downstairs and flung open the door, but no one was there. She looked down, and on the welcome mat sat a pair of brand new green high-tops, along with a note:

Dear Zibby,

Thank you for your offer to be in the Zibby and Sarah club. I accept.

I bought these shoes a while ago, hoping we could share them some day. If they fit, wear them tomorrow. I'll wear my tennies, and we can swap shoes when we see each other at school.

Sarah

Zibby ripped off her shoes, put on the high-tops, and laced them up.

They fit, she thought, admiring how they looked on her feet. *Perfectly!*

She started to step back inside when her mom appeared. She was dressed up in one of her best black dresses.

"There you are. I've been looking for you," she said. "I forgot to tell you earlier that we're leaving at six. That's in about twenty minutes."

"Leaving for where?"

"The restaurant," her mom said. "Tonight's the night we're taking Grandma Betty out for her birthday dinner. Remember?"

Zibby stared at her mom in disbelief. What with the Tomboy Club and everything else going on lately, she'd totally forgotten! And while for sure she wasn't going to wear that stupid dress, she only had a few minutes to find something decent to wear.

"I hope I can make it in time," she said to herself as she hurried past her mom and into her room.

CHAPTER 15

THE BEST IDEA OF ALL

Zibby threw the high-tops on her bed, then paced worriedly about her room. She had a clean pair of jeans to wear to dinner, but most of her T-shirts were in the wash. The only two that were clean were the oldest and rattiest ones Anthony had given her – a green one so faded it almost looked white, and a red baseball jersey with a rip in one sleeve.

"I don't think Grandma Betty would appreciate me wearing either of these," she said to herself.

She dug into her dirty clothes hamper, and smelled the T-shirts one by one under the arms. Unless she wanted to suffocate everyone at the table with "Eau d' Zibby," she couldn't wear any of them either.

"What am I going to do?" she asked herself, tapping her foot nervously.

I know, she thought. *Anthony will have to lend me one of his shirts. A good, clean one. Just for tonight. Then I'll give it back.*

She ran into Anthony's room, but then suddenly stopped in her tracks. There was Ashley standing next to

Anthony, looking through his CD collection! She was dressed in a blue pastel shirt, and a blue and white skirt. Anthony was wearing a button-down shirt, tie, and black dress pants.

"What are *you* doing here?" Zibby pointed at Ashley, her mouth hanging open.

"I'm going to dinner with you," Ashley replied, smiling.

"Mom said she could," Anthony said defensively.

"Oh," said Zibby, feeling totally unenthusiastic about the prospect. *Spending a whole night with Anthony and Ashley? Yuck*, she thought. Plus, with Ashley there, she was too embarrassed to ask Anthony for another shirt.

"Sorry, didn't mean to interrupt," she said, backing out of Anthony's room, eager to leave.

"Wait a minute," said Ashley. "Your brother tells me you like to play soccer."

"Yeah," Zibby said hesitantly.

"I play soccer," said Ashley. "For the high school team. I play right halfback. Didn't Anthony tell you that?"

"No," said Zibby, glancing at her brother, "but he's been pretty quiet around me lately."

Anthony shrugged his shoulders apologetically.

"Maybe one day we could kick the ball around in the backyard," said Ashley, "if you want to."

"Well, okay," said Zibby, suddenly smiling. "I could use some pointers. Thanks." And she hurried back to her room.

I guess if Ashley plays soccer, she can't be all that bad, she thought to herself. *And I would like to hear what it's like to be on the high school team. Maybe dinner won't be totally terrible – as long as I can get dressed in time!*

She sat down on her bed, nervously playing with the shoelaces of her new high-tops.

"What am I going to do?" she asked out loud, staring at the shoes.

And at that exact moment, Zibby was hit with her Best Idea Ever. An idea that fit in with her dad's – as well as her own – Theory of Flexibility, and that would have seemed impossible a week ago, but now felt right.

She ran into her parents' bedroom, opened her mom's closet, and found the backpacks and the suitcase that contained her clothes. She ripped open the first backpack, and frantically looked through its contents, and then moved on to the second backpack. And there she found what she was looking for.

Holding the garment in her hand, she raced back to her room, pulled off her dirty tomboy clothes, and pulled on the new outfit as well as some socks and shoes.

Next, she took off the beanie cap she'd been wearing all day, grabbed a brush off her dresser, and tried to make her hair look halfway decent without a hat. She was about to give up hope when she remembered the headband her mother had given her, which she'd set down on her desk. She slid it onto her head, and magically the bluntly cut bangs went neatly back.

She then stood in front of the mirror and gave herself a final check.

"There," she said to herself, satisfied by her reflection. "*Now* I'm ready."

Her parents were waiting for her in the living room as she made her way down the stairs. When they saw her, they gasped.

"Why, Elizabeth Mildred Payne, don't you look nice," her mom beamed at her. "You decided to wear the dress!"

Indeed she had. And even though Zibby felt pretty ridiculous wearing a frilly frock, it felt good to make her mom happy now, so she beamed right back. Besides, there was *something* about her outfit she definitely *did* like.

"Where's my little tomboy now?" asked her dad, smiling just as hard as her mom.

"She's still here," said Zibby. "You just have to look a bit harder to find her."

Actually, they didn't have to look all that hard. Because if her parents had taken a moment to look down at Zibby's feet, they would have noticed that underneath all the frills and bows, was a very new, very bright, and very wonderful flash of green.

THE END

PRINCE
CASPIAN

———◆———

C. S. Lewis

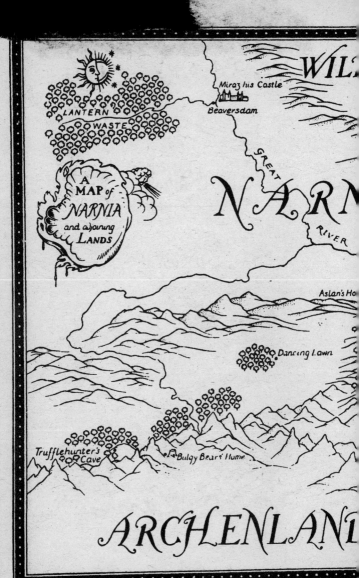

PRINCE
CASPIAN

C. S. Lewis

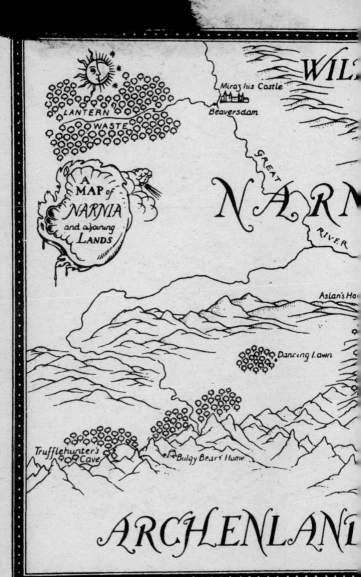

WIL

Miraz his Castle

Beaversdam

LANTERN

WASTE

GREAT

NARN

RIVER

A
MAP of
NARNIA
and adjoining
LANDS

Aslan's Ho

Dancing Lawn

Trufflehunter's
Cave

Bulgy Bears' Home

ARCHENLAND